ST MARY'S ABBEY

*Large oak tree
...was a
... and
...lace
...laws*

*Home of
Simon the Hermit*

*Caves which were the winter
quarters for the outlaws*

GISBORNE
CASTLE
*home of
Sir Guy
of Gisborne*

BARNSDALE

FOREST

*Church where Allen-a-dale
married the Lady Alice*

CASTLE WRANGBY
*home of the evil
Sir Isenbart de Belame*

Harold, the last of the Saxon kings, died at Hastings in 1066. Duke William of Normandy, the Conqueror, became King of England. The knights and lords who had supported him were rewarded with the rich Saxon manors and estates. The Church had supported William and so the monasteries also became rich and powerful.

For many years England was ruled harshly, not only by William but by the Norman kings who came after him. The Saxon freemen as well as the villeins (peasants) hated the new laws and taxes and felt bitterly towards their Norman masters.

There were few books in those days. Most men could not read and so the tales they heard were sung and told to them by travelling minstrels.

The hero of many of these stories was Robin Hood. Some of the ballads which were sung about him can be read from old manuscripts though over the years the stories have been altered and added to by many writers.

ROBIN HOOD
to the rescue

by DESMOND DUNKERLEY

with illustrations by BERNARD BRETT

Ladybird Books Loughborough

THE RESCUE

The early morning sun was just beginning to slant through the great oaks and beeches of Sherwood Forest. As autumn approached, the leaves were turning to gold and brown. The air was already warm with the promise of a fine October day. At the edge of the forest stood a rough, log hut. A cooking fire had been lit and smoke rose slowly through the trees. Only the hum of insects and the call of a wood pigeon broke the forest's silence.

Suddenly there was a cackling and flapping of wings. The woodcutter's wife ran from the hut waving a broom. She thought that a fox was after the chickens, but what she saw made her run back inside and bar the door.

An old woman looked up from the pot she was stirring. 'Was it a fox?' she asked. The two were alone, for the woodcutter had set out early for his work in the forest.

'What is it, I say?' asked the old woman again. Her voice was high and anxious now as she saw the expression on her daughter's face. 'A fox would not make you look so. Is it a wolf?' She got up and went to move back the window covering to look out, but the younger woman took her arm and held it firmly.

'Stay away, mother,' she said sharply. 'There's nothing we can do!'

'But a wolf is afraid of flames,' said the old woman. She freed her arm and seized a blazing branch from the fire.

'It's not a wolf, mother,' replied her daughter impatiently, 'it's . . .' She stopped and put her finger to her lips as there came the sound of blows and scuffling feet from just outside the door. They heard a frightened voice speak. 'Masters, what have I done that you should seize me like this?'

'What have you done, you Saxon knave?' growled a harsh Norman voice. 'Don't you know that the field where your geese were feeding is the lord's land? It's not common grazing for loutish Saxon villeins.'

'I suppose you thought that because this miserable place is half a day's ride from my lord's castle that you could get away with it!' said another voice roughly. 'But our lord Gisborne's patrols ride this far, and early, for he knows what thieving dogs you Saxons are!'

'Where's the harm?' cried the frightened voice again. 'The field is clear; the corn has been gathered! My geese were only feeding on the stubble to get them fat for Christmas.'

There was the sound of a blow then a cry of pain. 'Before you have your hand cut off for stealing,' said the Norman, 'perhaps twenty lashes in the castle tilting-yard will quiet your insolent Saxon tongue.' Still protesting, despite further blows, the captive was heard being led away.

When the sound of the voices grew fainter, the woodcutter's wife dared to open the door and peer out.

The two soldiers wore blue livery with a boar's head emblem. 'Two of the lord Gisborne's men, mother,' she whispered. 'They are taking old Goodman Price away with them. What shall we do?'

She watched in despair as the thin figure of the gooseherd was dragged across the clearing to where the soldiers had tethered their horses. A rope was attached to the villein's neck and the other end to a saddle pommel. His protests were cut short as the horses set off and the rope tightened.

'Gisborne!' said the old lady savagely. 'Curses on the Norman fiend! This would never have happened when Robert of Locksley was our master. Locksley lands were Saxon-owned and Saxon-run!'

'That's it, mother!' cried the girl excitedly. 'That's what we can do!'

'What, girl, what?' asked her mother.

'Robin Hood!' replied the girl excitedly. 'He will not stand by while one of his old servants is whipped and maimed.'

'No, he would not! But where will we find him?' asked her mother. 'Only the birds and the deer know where Robin Hood is to be found – or perhaps the little folk of the forest.'

'Hush, mother,' said the girl impatiently. 'This is not time for your goblin tales.'

Both of the women would have been terrified, however, had they seen the small brown figure flitting like a shadow through the trees.

'Simon the Hermit will know how to get word to Robin Hood if anyone does,' said the woodcutter's wife. 'First, Mistress Price must be told.' The old lady shuffled across the room to pick up her shawl from the table.

'No, you stay here, I can go more quickly on my own,' said the girl. She picked up her skirts, ran across the grass and into the trees.

She followed a well-worn path until she came to a small wooden hut with a thatched roof standing in a clearing. A few lean pigs were rooting about for acorns at the foot of the oak trees and a little old woman was bending over a small stream washing clothes. She looked up at the sound of running feet.

'You are in a hurry, neighbour!' she exclaimed. 'What's wrong?'

The woodcutter's wife was out of breath but she wasted no words. 'Betsy Price,' she panted, 'the soldiers – Sir Guy's soldiers – they've taken your man away – to be whipped – and worse I fear!'

Betsy Price gave a cry. 'Oh no!' she wailed. 'Not my poor man! What shall I do?' She hid her face in her apron and sobbed.

The woodcutter's wife knelt down and put an arm round the other's shoulders. 'We must somehow get word to Robin Hood,' she said.

'Master Robert!' said Betsy. 'Of course, he'll help. He knows us well from the old days. My man would have followed him to the greenwood when Locksley Hall was burned, but he was too old.' Then the sudden hope faded from the little lady's eyes and her face became doleful again.

'But where can we find him?' she wailed. 'He could be anywhere in the forest, and no one knows his hiding place.'

'We must try,' said the young woman firmly, helping the other to her feet. 'Old Simon will help if anyone can. Come, we must hurry.'

Deeper into the forest stood a great outcrop of limestone rock. The trees and undergrowth which grew all around it concealed the entrance to a large dry cave. It was here that Simon the Hermit lived. In the days when Robin Hood had been Robert of Locksley, a Saxon freeman and lord of all the lands in this part of Sherwood, Simon had been the priest at Locksley Hall.

When the Hall had been burned, its master had been forced to flee to the forest as an outlaw. Many of the younger villeins like Will Scarlet and Much the miller's son had followed him. Simon had been too old to go and had made his home in the cave which had been Robert's favourite hiding place when he was a child.

Others, like Goodman Price, had been too old for the hard and dangerous life of an outlaw and had been allowed to remain in their little huts by Sir Guy of Gisborne. He had been given all Locksley lands but as a Norman cared nothing for the Saxon peasants and treated them harshly and cruelly. He took what he wanted from them and left them little. Simon helped the peasants but he could not have done much without the daily visits from either Robin Hood or one of his men, bringing fresh meat, flour or clothes. Robin and his band roamed throughout Sherwood in their fight against Norman tyranny and injustice, but some of them were never far away from the outlaw leader's old home.

At this very moment, the hermit was talking to two men outside his cave. They wore Lincoln green, for although the leaves were changing there were still more green than gold, so the outlaws had not yet changed to their autumn russet and brown.

The taller of the two, a giant of a man, lowered the body of a wild boar from his shoulders while his companion spoke to Simon.

'You have heard nothing of this morning's trouble you say, old friend?'

'Nothing at all, Robin,' replied the hermit. 'It seems strange that word should have reached you before I knew of it.'

'Tull moves quickly when danger threatens, and he found us on our way here,' said Robin.

Simon nodded. Tull and his brother Caw were the little dark men of the woods. Each was no taller than a boy, and they lived in mounds deep in the forest somewhere. The superstitious villeins were frightened of them and called them goblins or brownies. Tull and his brother were devoted to Robin, who long ago had saved their lives. Now they acted as scouts, watchers and trackers for the outlaws.

Wherever Robin Hood was, night or day, at least one of the little men was never far away.

At that moment the three men looked up as the sound of a bell echoed through the trees.

'Perhaps we shall know now of this trouble,' said Simon. Little John swung the boar's carcase onto his shoulder again and followed Robin into the cave, while the hermit waited outside. When Locksley chapel had been burned, Simon had rescued the bell from the ruins, and now it hung high in the branches of an oak tree a little way from his cave. It was rung by the villagers when they wanted to see Simon, for he was often out gathering herbs or visiting the sick. It also served to give any of the hermit's visitors, who might not wish to be seen, time to hide inside the cave.

Betsy Price and the woodcutter's wife told Simon their tale of woe. They were unaware that the man whose help they needed was listening only a few feet away.

Meanwhile some miles away a small procession was making its way along the main forest track. The two Norman soldiers were riding slowly, for the sun was now warm. It was, nevertheless, a cruel way to travel for the old gooseherd who stumbled along behind them. He desperately tried to stop the rope around his neck from choking him.

Goodman Price was thankful to sink to the ground when two shepherds in long brown smocks and rough sheepskin jackets stopped the Normans to ask if they had seen any stray sheep back along the track. The shepherds received a surly reply and the taller one jerked his thumb at the pitiful figure of the gooseherd.

'What's he done then, master?'

'It's none of your business,' was the snarled reply, 'but he's to lose a hand for it, and a whipping first. That's what you'll get if you don't clear the path, you Saxon dolt!'

'I've never had a whipping, master,' said the tall shepherd. 'Have you?'

'You insolent oaf!' said the Norman. 'I've a mind to give you one now, with the flat of my sword.' He swung down from his horse and started to draw the blade. A sweeping blow on the wrist from the big shepherd's crook knocked the weapon from the Norman's hand. With a shout of rage he stooped to pick it up and received a second tremendous blow on his back which knocked him to the ground. Before the second soldier could recover from his surprise and help his comrade, he was dragged from the saddle by the other shepherd and given the same treatment. Goodman Price sat on the bank scarcely able to believe his eyes. The soldiers tried hard to fight back but soon their shouts and snarls of rage turned to moans and cries for mercy. At last the two shepherds stopped the punishment, though the giant one could not resist a last mighty blow.

'Now get you gone!' said the other sternly. 'Next time you start to drag an old man off to be whipped, remember what it feels like.'

The two soldiers staggered towards their horses. 'No!' said the shepherd. 'Leave the horses. Walk back to your evil den and think yourselves lucky that we don't ride and drag you along behind us, as you did this old man. Now, go!'

The two soldiers stumbled off along the track, groaning with pain. 'A last word, Norman bullies! Make sure in future that your patrol is wide of here, and that you don't seek this old man out again. Your faces are known and if either of you are seen in these parts you will surely die,' the shepherd called after them.

Robin Hood watched the two men-at-arms until they were out of sight. Then he and Little John retrieved their long bows, arrows and swords from the undergrowth where they had hidden them. They set Goodman Price on one of the horses and Robin mounted the other. Little John strode along beside them as they set off to see the old man safely home. The gooseherd tried to thank the two outlaws, whom he now recognised, but he found it difficult to speak. The rough rope had chafed his neck and made it sore.

'No thanks are needed, friend,' said Robin. 'You were loyal when times were good.'

It was early evening by the time the two outlaws left the old man outside his hut. They watched as he ran off happily.

Little John mounted the gooseherd's horse.

'Where now, Robin?' he asked. 'And what of these horses? They will be little use to us, and yet it seems a pity to set them loose to wander back to Gisborne's stables.'

'Yes, John,' replied Robin, 'we do not need them. A man can move faster and more quietly through the trees on foot. We'll send them to our friend, Sir Richard of the Lee, who will no doubt find a use for them. First we'll have a final gallop. I want to take a message to Sir Guy!'

It had taken the two men-at-arms all afternoon to reach Gisborne Castle. They were aching and sore from the beatings they had received and could only travel slowly. Unfortunately for them Sir Guy saw them trying to sneak in unobserved and had sent for them.

'By Saint Denis!' he roared angrily when he had heard their story. 'I cannot believe that two of my trained men could let themselves be beaten and whipped by a pair of doltish Saxon peasants! You'll pay for this insult at the whipping post! But first take others with you and burn out the . . .'

'My lord,' one of the soldiers interrupted, 'they were no . . .' Before he could finish he was struck by the furious Norman knight.

'Make no excuses, fool!' he roared. 'Do as I say or you will answer for it.'

The terrified soldier picked himself up and backed away from his angry master. His companion dared to make one last attempt.

'By your leave, my lord,' he mumbled, 'these were no ordinary peasants but . . .'

A drone like an angry hornet suddenly filled the room. It ended with a thud as a cloth-yard arrow sank into the wooden floor and stuck there quivering at Gisborne's feet. Only after he had bellowed orders to the two soldiers to turn out the guard and search the grounds, did Sir Guy read the tiny scroll of parchment wrapped round the arrow's shaft.

'Robin Hood!' he breathed. 'So those fools of mine were right. By all the saints, the time has come to rid me of this proud Saxon who dares to send me threats and tell a Norman where he may and may not ride.'

He stopped pacing furiously up and down and peered through the narrow window slit. The sun was setting, red and glowing in the western sky. By its light Sir Guy could just make out the line of

trees that marked the forest's edge beyond his
outer castle wall.

He looked again at the long arrow embedded in
the floor. Sir Guy of Gisborne shivered as he
realised that the master bowman whose shaft had
found its mark in that dim light was his deadly
enemy.

THE GHOST HORSE

Robin threw another branch onto the fire and it sent up a shower of sparks.

'Soon we shall need to move to our winter camp,' he said. He pulled his cloak more closely about his shoulders against the damp evening mist. 'The days are getting shorter and the nights colder.'

'Aye,' replied Will Scarlet, 'I suppose we must, but I don't like the thought, I must say. Those caves make a man feel shut in.'

'At least *you* can stand up straight in them without knocking your head,' groaned Little John.

'And you can get through the opening easily,' grumbled Friar Tuck. The outlaws who were gathered round the fire laughed as they thought of the discomfort of their two large comrades.

'I hate to leave the greenwood,' said Robin, 'but the leaves are nearly all gone from the trees. Our secret ways and places are now no longer hidden. Besides which, the moss and the grass on the banks are now much too damp for sleeping.' The outlaw leader stood up. 'We'll start to move tomorrow evening as soon as the sun sets,' he said. 'That gives us all day tomorrow to prepare and there are still two hours of light left to us tonight in which to start our preparations.'

Each autumn the outlaw band moved away from this part of Sherwood Forest. Here the trees and undergrowth grew thickly in spring and summer. To the north of Nottingham the ground became wilder, broken by cliffs and craggy outcrops of granite. The oaks and beeches of the south gave way to fir, spruce and larch. In the vast, tumbled rocks, well hidden by the evergreens, were many caves where the outlaws could be warm and dry throughout the autumn and winter months. In the spring they would return to their beloved greenwood.

There were many preparations to be made for the move. Although each man had very few belongings there was plenty to be moved which belonged to all of them. Their stores and equipment were kept carefully hidden in the trunks of hollow trees or in hollow logs with a curtain of growing bracken at either end.

Some of them were sitting on the banks from which they had scooped out the earth and lined the holes with stones.

'Friar,' said Robin, 'choose six lads to help you to gather together all our spare weapons. Dodd, see that you muffle the pots and pans well when they are bundled together so that they make no noise on the march. Much, the treasury boxes need to be well secured. Allen, will you see to the clothes and the bolts of cloth? Any of the brown homespun that we shall not need ourselves when we change from our summer green, take to old Simon. He will find a use for it this winter.'

The clearing became a bustle of activity and Robin called to Scarlet. 'Will, go round the sentries and tell them what's happening. Ask them to keep a special watch while we are so busy.'

Will Scarlet set off at a run and Robin turned to Little John.

'I'll go this evening to Sir Richard of the Lee,' he said. 'When we met last, I told him of this yearly move so that he would know where to look for us should he need our help before we return here in the spring. When Sir Richard heard how far we must travel with our belongings he offered pack horses from his stable to help ease our burdens.'

'May the saints preserve the thoughtful knight,' replied Little John. His burden on the march was always double that of anyone else. 'Shall I come with you, Robin?'

'No, John,' said Robin. 'Stay here in command and see that all is packed and ready. I'll ask Sir Richard to send the horses tomorrow with his steward and groom. Then I can be back by dawn.'

'Go carefully then, Robin,' warned Little John. 'The woods are full of Gisborne's spies. He is still smarting from the insult to his so-called Norman honour when we freed the gooseherd and whipped the varlets wearing his crest. I'll wager he did not like the note you sent him either, so, have a care.'

'I will, never fear,' said Robin. He clapped his tall lieutenant on the shoulder. 'Besides, you know I am never alone in Sherwood,' and he cupped his hands to his mouth to make the chirpy, challenging call of the blackcock. When no answering call came Robin looked puzzled and gave the cry again.

The bustle in the clearing stopped as all the outlaws waited and listened.

'Something's wrong, John,' said Robin urgently. 'Neither Tull nor Caw are close at hand. I must find out why before anything else.' Seizing his bow he turned to Little John again.

'If all is well with the Little Ones,' he said, 'I'll go on to Sir Richard's. If there is mischief afoot, as I fear, you'll hear my horn. Then come straight away for I shall need you. Pass word to the others.'

The outlaw leader made his way quickly through the dense forest. He knew the little tracks and paths better than anyone except perhaps the two little forest men whom he now sought. Once he had passed the last sentry and returned his greeting, Robin began to move more stealthily. His footfall made no sound on the soft leaves and no twigs snapped beneath his feet. He ducked below any overhanging branches so that his progress was as silent, yet as swift, as a hunting cat.

Robin was making for Two Barrow Bank in the heart of the forest. Here were the two green mounds beneath which Tull of the Hill and his brother Caw lived. It was already dusk as he approached the glade where the homes of the little men lay. He stopped at the edge of the trees and looked across the clearing at the dark outlines of the two long mounds.

Nothing moved. Robin stayed quite still, looking intently and letting his eyes adjust to the gathering darkness. An owl hooted, and then all was quiet again apart from the rustle of a rising breeze. Robin waited and was about to sound his blackcock call when he froze. He bent forward to peer even more intently at the nearer of the two mounds. A dark shape on its lower slope had just started to move. It was the figure of a man and by its size Robin knew that it was neither of the two brothers. As he watched, the figure began to wriggle upwards slowly, like a snake, towards the top of the hillock.

Robin feared to shoot lest the intruder was one of his own men. He had given orders that they were never to approach the mounds. Robin stepped forward quickly, sword in hand.

Suddenly he saw against the skyline, a small shape leap from the top of the mound on to the creeping form. They rolled down the slope in a wildly struggling heap. As Robin ran towards them he heard the fierce grunts of the two fighters, and saw in the moonlight the glint of steel. Just as he reached them he saw the smaller figure's arm raised high and stab down fiercely. There was a choking cry and a body rolled loosely down the slope until it lay sprawled lifelessly at Robin's feet. The outlaw saw with shocked surprise that the dead man wore Lincoln green.

'What's this, Caw?' he said angrily to the little man. 'Has one of my men dared to . . .?'

'Not one of your band, master,' panted Caw. He squatted down on the bank and cleaned his knife on the grass. 'He's a Gisborne spy. He killed your young Hal this morning, and took his green clothes for a disguise.'

'Poor Hal,' said Robin softly. 'But why did this carrion come here, and . . .?'

'I was on my way to give you warning,' said Caw. 'He followed me here'.

Robin knelt down and moved aside the little man's leather jerkin. 'How did you get this wound?' he asked, 'and what would you warn me of?'

'The Devil's loose in the forest,' said Caw.

'The Devil?' said Robin. He knew well to whom the little man referred. 'Gisborne's in Sherwood?'

'Aye, master, and more like this with him. I got the wound when they took Tull,' replied Caw.

'Tull a prisoner?' cried Robin leaping to his feet. 'Where is he held, and by how many?'

'The Devil and ten of his soldiers hold my brother at Outwoods,' said Caw. 'Like all Normans they fear the woods at night,' the little man went on scornfully, 'so they stay there until the morning when the help they've sent for will arrive. They think themselves safe there, and that no one knows their hiding-place. This thing here was meant to silence my tongue,' and he kicked the body of the dead spy once again.

'Then there is no time to lose,' said Robin urgently. He turned to face the way he had come and gave one long blast on his horn.

'I'll sound again when we are over by Outwoods,' he said. 'Are you fit to travel, Little One?'

'The Devil has my brother,' Caw answered simply. They both set off into the trees.

Outwoods was a stoutly-built timber hunting lodge like many in the king's deer forests. They were used only when the chase had carried a royal hunting party too far into the woods for them to return home the same night. At other times, only a steward would be there to keep the lodge ready for any unexpected royal visit. It was more than an ordinary man's life would be worth to stay in one of these royal lodges overnight, but Sir Guy of Gisborne was no ordinary man. He was a high-born Norman and a friend of Prince John, the king's brother, who ruled England in King Richard's absence.

As Robin Hood and his little companion moved rapidly through the woods, the outlaw stopped at intervals to sound his horn again to bring the outlaws in the right direction. When they could see the lodge by the light of the moon, Robin used the harsh cry of a nightjar instead, to bring his men to him. The horn's blast would have warned the Normans of their presence.

While Robin waited in a small clearing near to the lodge, Caw slipped away to scout. In ones and twos the outlaws joined Robin. He noticed with pride how even the clumsy villeins of a few months back were now as silent in the woods as any forest man. At length more than twenty were squatting silently around him.

'We had to leave the camp well guarded,' explained Little John in a whisper. 'It was full of all our goods. More are in readiness to come if you call them up.'

'We should have enough stout lads here to do what has to be done,' said Robin. 'Although there are barely enough of us to ring the house round as tight as I would have wished.' Then he told them what had happened.

'So the wolf has left his lair at last, and we have him,' growled Little John with deep satisfaction.

'Yes,' replied Robin, 'though we do not have him yet. Tull must be freed first, remember, and quietly. If the alarm is given the Little One will be the first to die.'

Out of the darkness a small dark figure appeared suddenly at his side. Some of the newer outlaws started in fear. 'How lies the land?' inquired Robin.

The Normans had taken few precautions. They believed that their captive's brother had been killed by the disguised spy and that their whereabouts were unknown. In the morning, the man-at-arms who had been despatched to Gisborne Castle would return with a large mounted force.

'Tull lies in the root cellar at the back, trussed like a pig,' said Caw. 'He knows we are here and will be ready. One mailed soldier guards him. Another watches the front. The Devil and all the rest are sleeping.'

Robin gave quick, whispered instructions and his men moved noiselessly away. The sentry at the back of the lodge saw or heard nothing. He felt only a second's blinding pain in his chest before slumping lifeless at Caw's feet. Robin embraced the freed Tull and received wordless thanks from the glowing dark eyes. Then the outlaw leader blew a resounding blast on his horn.

The sound brought an instant cry from the second sentry and shouted orders could be heard from inside.

'Gisborne!' cried Robin Hood. 'The time has come for you to pay for all your foul deeds!' Red flames leapt up around the door as the piled brushwood and bracken was set ablaze by Little John. 'Whether you come out and face me like the knight you claim to be, or burn in your hole like the wolf you are, matters not to us!'

A harsh shout of defiance was the only reply and then there was silence broken only by the crackling of the flames. Suddenly the great door of the lodge was flung open with a crash.

It scattered the burning brushwood and through it dashed the Norman soldiers. They shouted fiercely, with shields raised and weapons ready. The outlaws rushed to meet them hand to hand. The uncertain light and the confusion made shooting impossible. The fight raged fiercely in the clearing and amongst the trees for although outnumbered the Normans were trained soldiers who fought bravely. They knew they could expect no mercy. Greater numbers told in the end. The last mail-clad figure was cut down, and Robin looked amongst the dead bodies for his great enemy. Gisborne was not there, and Robin was about to dash into the burning lodge in search of him when two of his newest recruits came running from the back of the lodge. Their eyes were wide with fright and they cried in terror.

'The Ghost Horse, master, 'tis the Ghost Horse!' gasped Bat.

'What do you mean?' asked Robin sharply.

'It dashed out of the doorway there,' panted the other young outlaw. 'Its mane was all on fire and its eyes were flashing red. It was terrible!'

'I think the crafty knight has escaped!' said Robin. There was a roar of rage from the gathered outlaws.

'Nay, master, it was the Ghost Horse,' repeated Bat. 'Its great mouth was open to tear us to pieces.'

'Fool!' growled Little John. 'Villein you were, and villein you still are, with your stupid village superstitions!'

'Don't be too hard on them, John,' said Robin. He turned to the steward of the lodge who had taken no part in the fighting and had come out with his hands raised high.

'Tell me, fellow,' Robin said to the frightened man, 'has a horse been killed here recently?'

'Aye, master,' quaked the steward. 'The grey mare that my Lord Gisborne rode in on yesterday broke a leg and was finished off. The hide hangs in the store there, at the end of the house.'

'It's there no longer, I'll wager,' said Robin. Little John went off to find out. There were cries of rage from the outlaws when he returned empty-handed and they realised that they had been tricked.

'Never fear, lads,' called Robin. 'The wolf has escaped us now but his time will come. The night's work has not been wasted. Here are ten Norman knaves who will not harass honest villeins. Best of all, we freed the Little One.' He looked round for Tull, but neither he nor Caw were anywhere to be seen.

'They left together when they heard of Bat's Ghost Horse,' said Scarlet. Bat looked abashed and scuffled his feet as the other outlaws laughed wryly.

'And we had best be gone,' said Robin and looked up at the sky. 'Gisborne's mounted troop will be here before long.'

As they moved along the forest tracks to their camp, Robin remembered the move north.

'We'll have to go north without the horses, John,' he said. 'There's no time now to borrow them from Sir Richard, for the greenwood camp is broken and already packed.'

'It was pleasant to think of it for a while, though,' said Little John.

THE AMBUSH

Sir Guy of Gisborne barely escaped with his life. As soon as he had burst through the thin cordon of terrified outlaws, the Norman threw aside his horsehide disguise and his thin suit of chain mail so that he could move more quickly. Then he made straight for the main track through the forest hoping to meet the reinforcements he had sent for.

As Caw had rightly said to Robin, Normans did not like the woods at night. They disliked the huge darkness and the strange shapes made by the trees. Most of all they feared the sudden night noises. A Saxon forester would know the cry of a wild cat that had made its kill, or the screech of a hunting owl and the sudden scream that was the last cry of a stricken hare. To a Norman, these sounds were all strange and terrifying.

For all his cruelty, Gisborne was braver than most and paid little attention to any noises he heard. Yet he was thankful for the autumn moon which lightened the way, and helped him to travel more quickly. He felt the pursuit and the danger all around him though he could not see or hear it. He shivered slightly when he remembered the fierce hatred in the black glinting eyes of the little forest man who had been his captive. Then he cursed softly to himself as he thought of how all the secrets of Robin Hood's hiding places could have been wrung from the prisoner in the deep dungeons of Gisborne Castle.

The Norman's thoughts then centred with a deep and furious hatred on his arch enemy. He knew that his cruel and greedy ambitions could never be realised, and that his own life would never be safe, until Robin Hood was dead and his outlaw band broken and scattered.

Gisborne did not realise at first how close to death he himself was. Tull and Caw had found the discarded horsehide and chain mail suit. They had tracked the fleeing Norman to the main path. Now they were hunting him as swiftly and as silently as a cat hunts a mouse. Not until Tull and Caw were very close behind him did Gisborne hear them. Now fear took the place of rage. Though he knew that his sword would have hindered his escape he longed for it now. He cursed as he fumbled for the dagger in his belt.

Gisborne knew that he could run no further and leaned against a tree, breathing in great gasps of air. He looked back along the track, his dagger weaving circles in front of him ready for the sudden attack. He stiffened as he heard soft footsteps stop. Two small figures stood together in the moonlight for a moment before separating, gliding off into the bushes at either side. The sudden bark of a hound that has sighted its quarry came from the blackness to Gisborne's left. He swung round to face it but turned back as the call was answered from the other side. The wolf was at bay.

The expected attack never came. Another cry, the warning bark of a fox, sounded from his left and was at once answered. Seconds later Gisborne, too, heard the hoof beats of many horses as his Norman troop rode to his rescue.

Gisborne knew that his pursuers would have faded away into the darkness. Robin Hood and his men would long since have left the Outwoods. There was an angry glow in the sky as Gisborne headed his troop back to the castle. His mind was already planning ways in which the outlaws could be found and destroyed.

The cavalcade clattered across the drawbridge as dawn was breaking.

'In the devil's name, what is this?' demanded Gisborne savagely. His steward had run up to hold his master's horse. 'Has Gisborne Castle become a wayside hostelry? What's afoot, knave?'

Two dozen heavily laden packhorses were jostling and stamping their hooves in the courtyard. As many black gowned monks supervised the servants who were starting to unload the heavy wooden chests that each animal carried.

'No, my lord,' replied the frightened steward. ''Tis an abbot, my lord, on his way to found a new abbey in these parts. These are all his goods.'

'A plague on all his goods, and on his new abbey,' snarled the knight. He flung his reins to a groom. 'Tell the fool to come to me!'

'He brings a letter for you from Prince John, my lord,' said the steward.

'Does he, by thunder!' exclaimed Gisborne. 'A well connected abbot! Then you had best ask and not tell. Go, dolt, and send food and wine also!'

It was nearly mid-morning before the abbot's pack train left the castle. By noon it had crossed the common land, passed by all the strips and the cultivated land and was through the outer thickets and undergrowth of the woods.

By early evening it was deep into Sherwood Forest.

Will Scarlet saw it first from high in the branches of an oak tree where he was keeping watch.

'We're in luck, John!' he called down to his companion on the ground. 'One last haul, if Robin wants it, before we move north.'

Showing great agility for a man of his size, Little John climbed up to join Will Scarlet.

'Look at all those chests,' said Scarlet. He imagined all the gold they might contain.

'Never mind the chests, look at those lovely horses,' replied Little John, happily. He thought of the long trek to the northern caves which faced them that evening.

For a moment longer the two outlaws watched the long line of pack animals and their attendant monks winding along the narrow path. Then they quickly climbed down and ran to report to Robin.

Although Sir Guy of Gisborne had warned him what to expect, the abbot was very frightened when a tall figure in green stepped out onto the track in front of his horse.

'Hold, Sir Abbot!' called Robin Hood. 'There is a toll to be paid by all who would pass this way.'

Terrified though he was, the abbot remembered to play his part as he had been instructed.

'Toll, you knave? What toll is this, and who are you?' he demanded with as much bluster as he could manage.

'I am Robin Hood, whom men call King of Sherwood,' was the reply. 'A toll is paid to guarantee safe passage through these parts until King Richard is home to make them safe again. Fear not, Sir Abbot, I only take half of all you carry. The rest I will leave here beside the road for you to collect. I need to borrow your fine horses for a while.'

Gisborne had warned the abbot that it was the outlaws' custom not to take all a traveller's goods and money. This would not suit Gisborne's plan.

'Take it all, you rogue, and the horses, too,' said the frightened abbot. He had now had enough and wanted to be gone. He gathered his robes about him and scurried off down the track followed by his frightened monks. Robin looked after the fleeing figures in surprise.

'That was strange behaviour, John,' he said. The other outlaws emerged from the undergrowth on either side and joined their leader. 'No rage and only a little bluster. No threats of punishment and all their goods left without a word of argument.'

'And all their horses!' said Little John with satisfaction.

'And no one but me in sight,' went on Robin. 'Strange indeed. What do you think, Tuck? Allen? Will?'

'Abbots are usually full of huff and puff,' said Friar Tuck, 'yet this one was not.' He walked up to the first horse and stroked its long nose thoughtfully. 'It could be that . . .' He stopped talking for a moment to peer more closely at the large wooden chest on the horse's back. Then he started talking again about abbots and their ways. All the time he beckoned Robin to join him. He pointed at the chest. Robin looked at it quickly, examined the one on the other side and then walked away to where the outlaws stood.

He whispered a few instructions to them then called loudly, 'Right, lads. The good abbot does not want his share, and kindly lets us borrow his horses. Each take a bridle and we will lead them, with the treasure, to our camp.'

The cavalcade set off along the path. Each horse was led by an outlaw who carried a knife in his other hand. Another outlaw walked alongside carrying his bow with an arrow notched to the string.

They came at last to a wide stream which ran through the forest before joining the River Trent some miles away. The outlaws led the horses to where the stream was at its widest and deepest.

The horses were sent into the water with a slap and the ropes holding the chests were slashed free. As the horses careered into the stream the chests were jolted loose from their wooden cradles. They fell into the water and started to float downstream, turning lazily in the current.

Then water began to pour into them through the many holes bored in their sides which the keen eyes of Friar Tuck had spotted. Some turned over altogether and sank. From the others came shouts of rage and fear as the lids were forced open and a Norman man-at-arms tried to scramble from each one.

Most only managed to capsize their clumsy
chests to find themselves floundering downstream.
A few succeeded in clambering ashore with their
hands held high in surrender. Only one came up
with sword in hand. He dashed at Robin snarling,
to be cut down by an arrow from Will Stuteley's
bow.

'Go back to your master,' Robin said sternly to the survivors, 'and tell him that the arm of Robin Hood is long and that Saxon vengeance is sure. Tell him that his days are numbered and that his life is forfeit for his evil deeds. Go now!'

The frightened men-at-arms stumbled away. They were glad to be alive, though fearful of their master's fury when they returned. Meanwhile Little John, with some help, had collected up the horses and was happily leading them back to camp.

One of the two small figures who had watched all from their hiding place gave the shrill triumphant cry of a hawk. Robin Hood smiled as he turned and raised his hand to the thickly-spreading yew tree from which the sound came.

LOCKSLEY HALL

where Robin live
before it was bur
down and he beca
an outlaw

COPMANHU
Robin Hood m
Friar Tuck

SHERWOOD
FOREST

This picture has been based on a map of Nottingham
and the Sherwood forest area. It shows where some of
the events in the stories may have taken place and
where some of the places mentioned in the books
might have been situated.

Log over the stre
where Little John
fought Robin Hoo

OUTWOODS HUNTING LODGE

Mounds which were t
home of Tull and Cav

Main summer quarters for
Robin Hood and his men

NOTTINGHAM CASTLE
home of the Sheriff
of Nottingham

to ASHBY